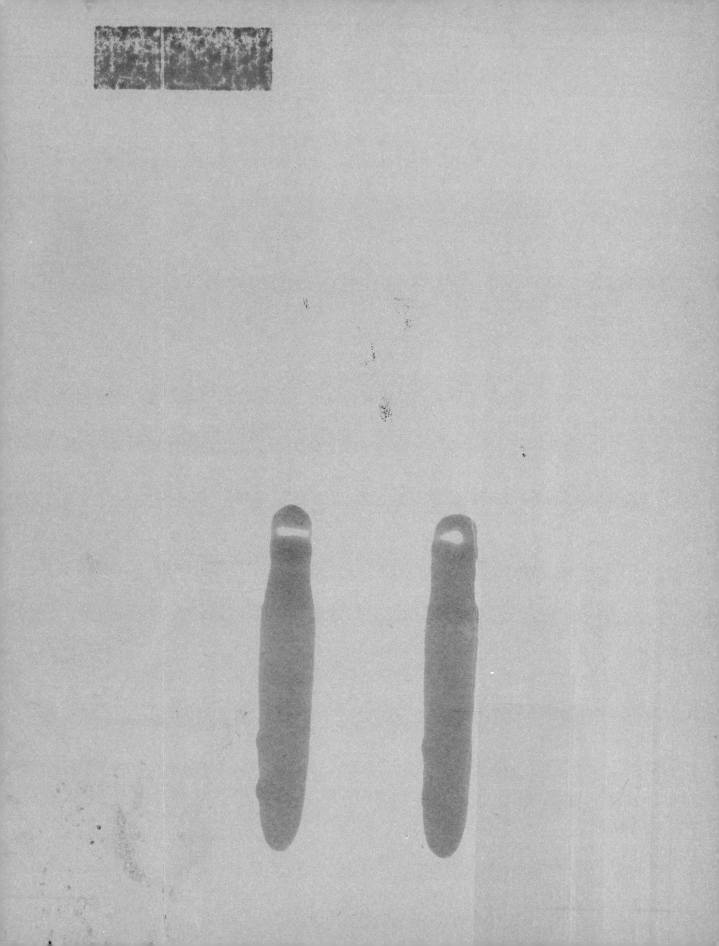

When Summer Ends

by SUSI GREGG FOWLER

pictures by

MARISABINA RUSSO

 Greenwillow Books, New York

For my daughters, Angela
and Micaela, and for Jim,
who nurtures us all.
With love —
—S. G. F.

For Thérèse and Patti,
Steph, and Aunt Joanne
—M.R.

Gouache paints were used for the full-color art.
The text type is ITC Mixage Medium.

Text copyright © 1989 by Susi L. Gregg Fowler
Illustrations copyright © 1989 by
Marisabina Russo Stark

Printed in Hong Kong by South China Printing Co.

First Edition
10 9 8 7 6 5 4 3 2 1

Library of Congress Cataloging-In-Publication Data
Fowler, Susi Gregg.
When summer ends.
Summary: A young child is sorry to see
summer end until she remembers all the
good things the other seasons bring.
[1. Seasons—Fiction]
I. Russo, Marisabina, ill.   II. Title.
PZ7.F8297Wh   1989   [E]   87-14937
ISBN 0-688-07605-X
ISBN 0-688-07606-8 (lib. bdg.)

When summer ends I will cry and cry.

Why?

Because everything good happens in summer.

Like what?

Like the Fourth of July,
and watermelon,
and splashing in the
front yard pool,

and cousins coming—
and frogs and flowers—
and berries and
wearing shorts!

What about autumn?

I don't like autumn.

What about Halloween?

Oh.

What about piles of
crisp leaves to jump in?

Oh.

And the first frost, and fires in
the fireplace, and Thanksgiving
turkeys, and pumpkin pies?

Oh.
I guess I like autumn.

What about winter?

I don't like winter.

What about Christmas?

Oh.

What about building fat snowmen,
and tasting snowflakes, and being
so bundled up even Grandma doesn't
know who you are?

Oh.
I guess I like winter.

What about spring?

I don't like spring.

What about Easter?

Oh.

What about watching
the geese come back?

Oh.

And pussy willows, and flying your kite, and flowers poking through the snow,

and lots of puddles everywhere,
and new boots for wading?

Oh.
I guess I like spring.

When will summer be over?

Soon. Why?

Because nothing good
ever happens in summer.